Jamie Lee Curtis & Laura Cornell

It's Hard to Be Five

Learning How to Work My Control Panel

Joanna Cotler Books

An Imprint of HarperCollins Publishers

I would like to give a HIGH FIVE to Joanna and Laura,
my creative comrades, Phyllis, Kelly, Justin, Melissa, Alicia,
Lucille and everyone at HarperCollins and a Special Everest
HIGH FIVE to Thomas—just for being you.
—J.L.C.

I am grateful for the quintet that surrounds and makes me—
Jamie, Joanna, Justin, Melissa and Alicia—
and beyond—all at the great HarperCollins.
—L.C.

It's Hard to Be Five: Learning How to Work My Control Panel
Text copyright © 2004 by Jamie Lee Curtis   Illustrations copyright © 2004 by Laura Cornell
Printed in the U.S.A.   All rights reserved.   www.harperchildrens.com
Library of Congress Cataloging-in-Publication Data   Curtis, Jamie Lee.   It's hard to be five : learning how to
work my control panel / by Jamie Lee Curtis & Laura Cornell.— 1st ed.   p. cm.
Summary: A child finds that learning to have self-control is hard, but it can also be fun.
ISBN 0-06-008095-7 — ISBN 0-06-008096-5 (lib. bdg.)   [1. Growth—Fiction. 2. Stories in rhyme.]
I. Title: It is hard to be five. II. Cornell, Laura, ill. III. Title.   PZ8.3.C9347It 2004   2003024187   [E]—dc22
Designed by Alicia Mikles   1 2 3 4 5 6 7 8 9 10   First Edition

For Robert Brandt, my dad
—J.L.C.

For Barbara and Neal who gave me
the best and easiest "5 years old"
—L.C.

It's **hard** to be five.
I'm little no more.
Good old days are gone.
'Bye

one,

two,

three,

four.

It's hard to be five. Just yelled at my brother.

My **mind** says do one thing,

my **mouth** says another.

Would you ever so kindly please give me my wig back?

Perhaps an offer of just a small taste would be nice.

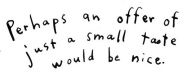

Let's see. It's been an hour and nine minutes. Might I have a smidge of a turn before we have to leave?

IT's MINE!

Give iT! MOM!

It's hard to be five. I've got to keep going.
My clothes can't keep up 'cause my body keeps growing.

At five I hear **NO** and **DON'T**—I can't win!—
when balls bowl inside at my ten juice-box pins.

I'd rather hear **TRY IT** and **SURE,** I confess . . .

. . . and if dirt is involved, a very loud

It's hard to be five.
Parents want you all clean.

It's hard to be five.
All I want is to play.
I'm starting at school,
and I don't get a say.
School seems so scary.
School seems so strange.
I'm only five.
My whole world's going to change.

It's hard to be five and wanting to hit
when Scott **cuts** in line and says **I** did it.

At five I do things that I don't mean to do,
like when I **bit** Jake 'cause **he** cut in line too.

It's hard to be five. It takes Superman skill. Sitting in circles. Sitting so still.

Sitting still.

Still sitting still.

 Still

 Sitting

 Still.

SIT STILL!

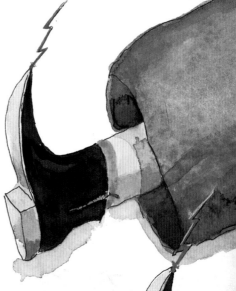

And then there's the **walking** all by myself, only picked up to reach a high shelf.

I walk to the park.

I walk to the school.

I walk to the bus.

I walk to the pool.

I walk to karate.
I walk with closed eyes.

I walk like
a ninja

chopping
bad guys.

It's **fun** to be five! **Big** changes are here!

My body's my car,
and I'm **licensed** to steer.

At five I'm a worker—a bee among bees.

I build things and grow things, say thank you and please.

Some **fun** things are hard.

And some **hard** things are fun.

I know when to **walk.**

I know when to **run.**

I know when to **stop**.

And I know when to **go**.

I know when to **push**.

And I know when to **tow**.

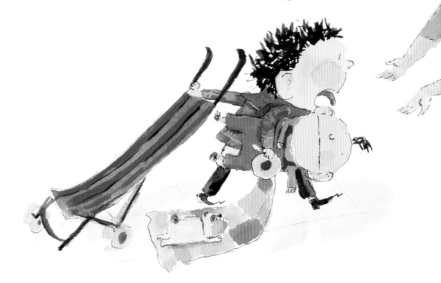

At five I can lie down alone in my bed
and dream of my past and my future ahead.
And when I mess up or do right, it's a start,
'cause I have my own mind
and I have my own heart.

It's hard **fun** to be five

fun

to be
five

so **strong**
and so **loud.**